LITTLE RED RIDING HOOD

Adapted from the Retelling by the Brothers Grimm

PAUL GALDONE

A FOLK TALE CLASSIC

Houghton Mifflin Harcourt

Boston   New York

To Amy Spaulding

All rights reserved. Published in the United States by HMH Books, an imprint of
Houghton Mifflin Harcourt Publishing Company. Originally published in hardcover
in the United States by the McGraw-Hill Book Company, 1974.

For information about permission to reproduce selections from this book, write to
trade.permissions@hmhco.com or to Permissions, Houghton Mifflin Harcourt
Publishing Company, 3 Park Avenue, 19th Floor, New York, New York 10016.

www.hmhco.com

Library of Congress Cataloging-in-Publication Control Number 74-6426

ISBN: 978-0-547-66855-0 paper over board

Manufactured in China
SCP 10 9 8
4500751106

Once

upon a time there was a sweet little maiden who was loved by all who knew her. She was especially dear to her grandmother, who did not know how to make enough of the child. Once she gave her a little red velvet cloak. It was so becoming and she liked it so much that she would never wear anything else. So she got the name of Little Red Riding Hood.

One day her mother said to her, "Come here,
Little Red Riding Hood! Take this cake and
bottle of wine to Grandmother. She is weak and ill,
and they will do her good.
Go quickly before it gets too hot.
Don't loiter along the way, nor run, or you will fall
and break the bottle, and there will be no wine for
Grandmother. When you get there, don't forget
to say 'Good morning' prettily, without staring about you."

"I will do just as you tell me,"
Little Red Riding Hood promised her mother.

Her grandmother lived away in the wood,
a good half hour from the village.
When she got to the wood she met a wolf,
but Little Red Riding Hood did not know what a wicked
animal he was, so she was not a bit afraid of him.

"Good morning, Little Red Riding Hood," he said.
"Good morning, wolf," she answered.

"Whither away so early, Little Red Riding Hood?"
"To Grandmother's."
"What have you got in your basket?"
"Cake and wine. We baked yesterday, so I am taking
a cake to her. She wants something to make her well."

"Where does your grandmother live, Little Red Riding Hood?"

"A good quarter of an hour farther into the wood.
Her house stands under three big oak trees near a
hedge of nut trees which you must know,"
said Little Red Riding Hood.

The wolf thought, "This tender little creature will be a plump morsel! She will be nicer than that old woman. I must be cunning and snap them both up."

He walked along with Little Red Riding Hood for a while.
Then he said, "Look at the pretty flowers,
Little Red Riding Hood. Why don't you look about you?
I don't believe you even hear the birds sing.
You are as solemn as if you were going to school.
All else is so gay out here in the woods."

Little Red Riding Hood raised her eyes, and when she saw the sunlight dancing through the trees, and all the bright flowers, she thought, "I'm sure Grandmother would be pleased if I took her a bunch of fresh flowers. It is still quite early. I shall have plenty of time to pick them."

So she left the path and wandered off among the trees to pick the flowers. Each time she picked one, she always saw another prettier one farther on. So she went deeper and deeper into the forest.

In the meantime
the wolf went straight off
to the grandmother's cottage
and knocked on the door.
"Who is there?"
"Little Red Riding Hood, bringing you
a cake and some wine.
Open the door!"

"Lift the latch,"
    called out the old woman.
"I am too weak to get up."

The wolf lifted the latch
and the door sprang open.
He went straight in
and up to the bed
without saying a word,
and ate up the poor old woman.

Then he put on
her nightdress and cap,
got into the bed and
drew up the curtains.

Little Red Riding Hood picked flowers till she could carry no more, and then she remembered her grandmother again. She was astonished when she got to the house to find the door open, and when she entered the room everything seemed strange.

She felt quite frightened but she did not know why.

"Generally I like coming to see Grandmother so much," she thought.

"Good morning, Grandmother," she cried.

But she received no answer.

Then she went up to the bed and drew the curtains back. There lay her grandmother, but she had drawn her cap down over her face and looked very odd.

"Oh Grandmother, what big ears you have," she said.
"The better to hear you with, my dear."
"Grandmother, what big eyes you have."
"The better to see you with, my dear."
"What big hands you have, Grandmother."
"The better to catch hold of you with, my dear."
"But Grandmother, what big teeth you have."
"The better to eat you with, my dear."

Hardly had the wolf said this
when he made a spring
out of bed and swallowed
poor Little Red Riding Hood.

A huntsman went out past the house and thought,
"How loudly the old lady is snoring.
I must see if there is anything
the matter with her."

So he went into the house and up to the bed,
where he found the wolf fast asleep.
"Do I find you here, you old sinner!" he said.
"Long enough have I sought you!"

He raised his gun to shoot,
when it just occurred to him
that perhaps the wolf had
eaten up the old lady,
and that she might
still be saved.

So he pulled the sleeping wolf's mouth wide open. The first thing
he saw was the little red cloak. The little girl sprang out and
cried,

"Oh, how frightened I was!
It was so dark inside the wolf." Next the old grandmother came,
alive but hardly able to breathe.

The wolf awoke and tried to spring up,
but he was so frightened
by the sight of the hunter
that he fell down dead.

They were all quite happy now. The huntsman took the dead wolf home.

The grandmother ate the cake and drank the wine that Little Red Riding Hood had brought, and she soon felt quite strong.

Little Red Riding Hood thought to herself, "I will never again wander off into the forest as long as I live, when my mother forbids it."